DISNEY'S
WINNIE THE POOH
Thanksgiving

by Bruce Talkington

illustrated by
John Kurtz

DISNEY
PRESS
NEW YORK

Disney's

WINNIE THE POOH'S
Thanksgiving

But where can he be?" Rabbit said in his most frustrated I-really-want-to-know voice.

It was the question that was in the mind of everyone standing at Winnie the Pooh's front door. The thoroughly frazzled Rabbit once again rapped loudly on the door, which continued to stand unopened no matter how vigorously he applied his knuckles.

Tigger was sitting back on his tail with his face flattened against the glass of Pooh's window.

"There's nothin' movin' in there," he informed the others.

"That doesn't mean a great deal," rumbled Eeyore from where he was seated on a nearby patch of grass. "Not movin' is one of the things Pooh Bear does best. Next to snoring."

"And eating honey," added little Roo excitedly. "Isn't that right, Mom?"

"Yes, dear," Kanga said as she smiled down at him and gently straightened his hair with her hand.

"Why would Pooh ask us here if he were somewhere else?" whistled Gopher, scratching his head.

Piglet stood wringing his very small hands worriedly. "Oh dear," he sighed, "I do hope he's all right."

"Now let's not jump to conclusions," Kanga spoke up gently, and Tigger wondered why ever not, because jumping was something he thoroughly enjoyed. But, he supposed, conclusions must be a little like Rabbit—they're not particularly pleased when people jump at them.

"If I remember correctly," Kanga continued, "Pooh Bear simply asked us to meet him. He didn't mention where."

"Very nice of him, too," remarked Eeyore. "He obviously didn't want us to feel bad if we couldn't find the right place, so he kept the location a secret."

"But we're makin' progress," hooted Tigger. "We know for sure it isn't ex-zack-tackily *here!*" And he pointed to the door.

"Now," Rabbit sighed, "if we could only think of the place where Pooh *is!*"

"Perhaps you just did," rumbled Eeyore. "Pooh was certainly thinking about something when he called us together . . ."

". . . an' Pooh boy always does his best head work . . . ," continued Tigger.

"... in his very own Thoughtful Spot!" finished Piglet.
And that is ex-zack-tackily where they found Winnie
the Pooh, high atop the grassy knoll, with its spectacular
view of the Hundred-Acre Wood and the beautiful blue
sky hanging high above it, where Pooh loved to sit and
think. It was the *sitting* in such a special place that was
important, after all, not the *thinking*.

Therefore, it was no surprise at all when Pooh was
found up there doing precisely that—*sitting* and looking
thoughtful. And there was no doubt as to what Pooh was
being thoughtful about. It was all spread out on a blanket
before him. Pooh's pantry must have been completely
emptied because everything sweet and tasty had been

toted from his house to the grassy knoll and arranged to look its most delicious.

"I'm so very glad you've come," sighed Winnie the Pooh happily. "I don't think this food could have waited much longer.

"And neither could I," he added with a smile.

"Then let's not waste a moment more," announced Rabbit, and they all sat down to eat.

"I'm very glad to see you at last," said Pooh. "I hope I haven't brought too much to eat."

"No such thing as too many eats when eatin' is the name o' the game," chuckled Tigger as he happily rubbed his paws together.

"Is eating the only reason you called us together, Pooh Bear?" asked Owl.

"Called you together where?" responded Pooh, tucking his tongue carefully into the corner of his mouth as he pulled the stopper on a fresh crock of honey because, as everyone knows, a stopper cannot be properly pulled if a tongue is not tactfully tucked.

"Why, called us *here*, Pooh," squeaked Roo.

"Did I do that?" said Pooh, so surprised by the idea that he waited an extra second or two before pouring an extra-large dollop of honey into his mouth.

"You certainly did," answered Gopher. "An' what we want to know is why you did it!"

"Not that it wasn't an excellent idea, Pooh dear," Kanga added gently.

"Well," murmured Pooh in a thoughtful sort of voice as he gently tugged on an ear with his honey-smeared

paw, "it must have begun this morning when I sat down for breakfast."

Pooh explained how he was suddenly very much aware of how special a breakfast could be because, like so very many things—sunsets and birthdays, surprises and nap times, hugs and extra dessert—a breakfast was more than

just today. It was an always-there-when-a-bear-needed-it sort of thing.

"You mean you were *grateful*, Pooh?" asked Piglet in a very quiet voice when his friend had finished.

"Why, yes, Piglet," smiled Pooh. "That's it exactly. And it was such a wonderful thank-you-very-much feeling, and

so very, *very* large, that I knew it was something I had to share with those I'm most grateful for."

"And what sort of 'those' do you mean, Pooh?" wondered Owl.

"Why, you all, of course," exclaimed Pooh. "My very best and dearest friends!"

"Well," sniffed Rabbit, "I'm certainly grateful that you thought of it."

"And what are *you* grateful for, Piglet?" Pooh inquired politely as he put his arm around his friend's very small shoulders.

"Well," began Piglet nervously, and then continued in a rush, "for a very small animal, I have a great deal to be grateful for. And having a lot to be grateful for is, when

you come right down to it, a *lot* to be grateful for!" Piglet finished quite out of breath.

When the question of gratitude was put to Rabbit, he explained that what he was primarily thankful for (besides his many very good friends, of course) was that a seed had the extremely good sense to sprout when he planted it in his garden.

"I'm grateful that the ground looks as good from

underneath as it does from on top," whistled Gopher. "Yes sirree!"

Tigger expressed his gratitude that down-ing through the air was just as splendiferous as up-ing.

"The item for which I am, indeed, most thankful," announced Owl in his most dignified voice, "is that I always remember in the nick of time to land on my feet and *not* on my face."

"I'm grateful just for the chance to be grateful," rumbled Eeyore. "If that's all right with everyone, that is."

Everyone agreed that it was, indeed, quite all right with them.

Kanga and little Roo said they were grateful for each other at exactly the same time.

And at that very moment Christopher Robin arrived

quite out of breath and said, "I'm terribly sorry to be so late, Pooh Bear. What exactly are we all doing up here?"

"We're having a feast and telling each other what we are grateful for," said Pooh.

Then Pooh surveyed the blanket and realized that there wasn't a single smackeral of anything left to eat.

"You missed the feast part, I'm afraid," he told Christopher Robin sadly.

"That's all right," laughed Christopher Robin. "I can still do the other."

Then he stood up straight and began to speak in a very grown-up voice.

"I'm very grateful for having the opportunity of finding you all here together so I can invite you to join me for Thanksgiving dinner."

"Thanksgiving dinner!" exclaimed everyone all at once. "What's that?"

"Well, you all already know the most important part," laughed Christopher Robin. "It's a special time when all the things we're grateful for throughout the year have their very own day to celebrate with us!"

"What a nice idea," said Pooh with a satisfied smile. "I'd like to thank whoever thought of it."

"You thought of it all by your lonesome, buddy bear," shouted Tigger as he slapped Pooh happily on the back.

"Ah," said Pooh with a grin, "the dinner part did sound familiar. And you did mention . . . dinner?" Pooh asked carefully.

"All you can eat . . . and *more*," Christopher Robin assured him.

"Isn't it wonderful," said Pooh as he rubbed his tummy, "that Thanksgiving dinner is something we're all warmed up for?"

Everyone agreed that it was, indeed, quite wonderful.

"Another thing," said Pooh quietly, "to be so very grateful for."